SCUBA LTD.

To the Cuckoo Cloots

First edition published in 2021 by Flying Eye Books,
an imprint of Nobrow Ltd. 27 Westgate Street, London, E8 3RL.

Text and Illustrations © Ricky Trickartt 2021

Ricky Trickartt has asserted his right under the Copyright, Designs and
Patents Act, 1988, to be identified as the Author and Illustrator of this Work.

1 3 5 7 9 10 8 6 4 2

Published in the US by Nobrow (US) Inc.
Printed in Poland on FSC® certified paper.

ISBN 978-1-838740-30-6
www.flyingeyebooks.com

RICKY TRICKARTT

ALLEY CAT RALLY

FLYING EYE BOOKS

LONDON · NEW YORK · KIBBLE HILL

when a noise came rumbling down the alley.

'Watch out, slowpoke!'

'How rude!', thought Asta,
when a sign caught her eye.

'If I had a racing car, I'd show them who's slow!'

Back at home, Asta was still thinking about the racers
when she came up with an idea.

She got straight to work on her machine.

Before she knew it, she had finished her racing car.

TWEET TWEET!

TWEET TWEET!

TWEET

TWEET TWEET!

On Thursday morning, Asta took her new machine for a test drive.

It took a lot of testing,

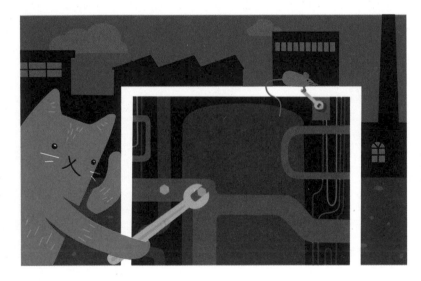

but eventually...

...it *whizzed* down Mount Tuna Road!

On Friday night, Asta could hardly sleep.

She got up early Saturday morning,
and was the first racer at the starting line.

Marvin **fidgeted** in his souped-up shopping trolley.

Cheese Denise had a need for **speed**!

Anton **purred** in his classic racer.

Is that Ludlow in some kind of **vegetable**?

Professor Kim had **science** on her side.

And Whiskers hoped to win with **paw-power**!

The racers all lined up and were ready to go.

'Start your engines!'

The racers **zoomed**
like the
Cheetah Express.

It was a close call for Ludlow
and the Professor at the duck pond.

Marvin was catching up to Whiskers by the factory.

Then just as the race was getting close,

Marvin took a wrong turn at the supermarket

and **crashed** into another shopping trolley!

The gap was increasing on the final bend.

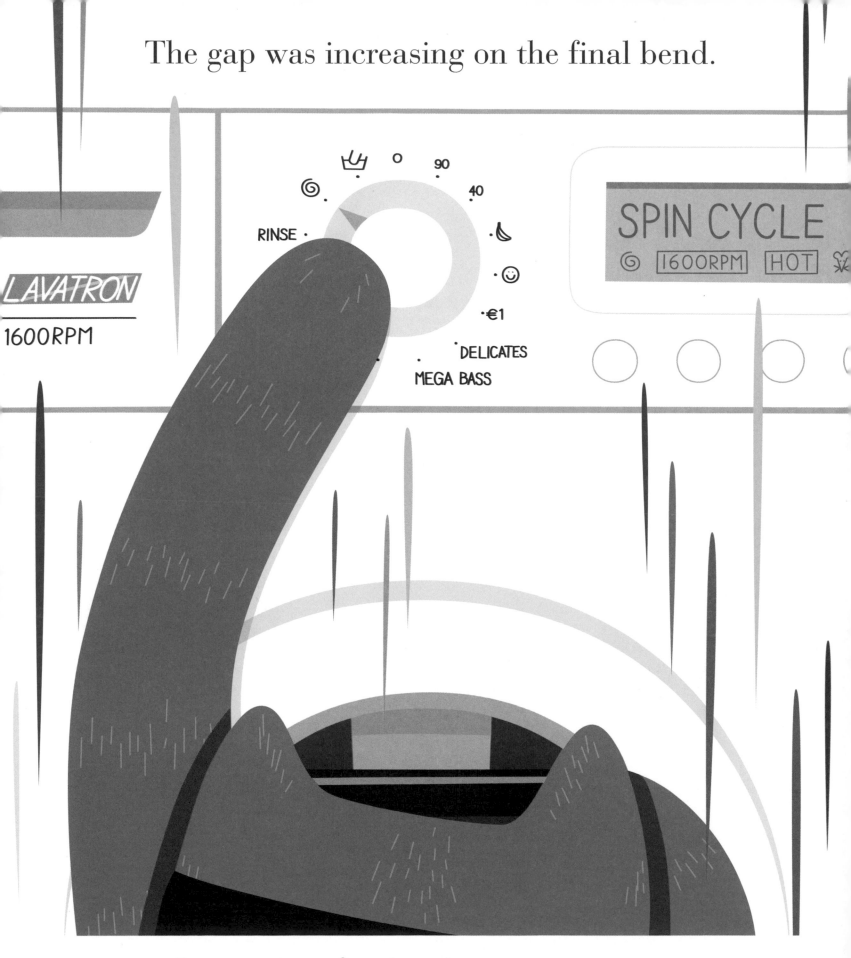

It was time for Asta's secret weapon...

WARP SPEED!

It was a photo finish at the line.

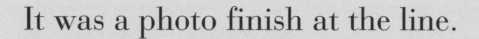

Asta won by a whisker!

'Wow! Asta is really fast!'

The alley cats apologised.
'We underestimated you, Asta!'

And they celebrated together
until even the moon wanted to go to sleep.

Then Asta woke up.

There are mice hiding all over this book, inside and out. Can you find them all?